WELCOME TO
PASSPORT TO READING
A beginning reader's ticket to a brand-new world!

Every book in this program is designed to build read-along and read-alone skills, level by level, through engaging and enriching stories. As the reader turns each page, he or she will become more confident with new vocabulary, sight words, and comprehension.

These PASSPORT TO READING levels will help you choose the perfect book for every reader.

READING TOGETHER
Read short words in simple sentence structures together to begin a reader's journey.

READING OUT LOUD
Encourage developing readers to sound out words in more complex stories with simple vocabulary.

READING INDEPENDENTLY
Newly independent readers gain confidence reading more complex sentences with higher word counts.

READY TO READ MORE
Readers prepare for chapter books with fewer illustrations and longer paragraphs.

This book features sight words from the educator-supported Dolch Sight Words List. This encourages the reader to recognize commonly used vocabulary words, increasing reading speed and fluency.

For more information, please visit passporttoreadingbooks.com.

Enjoy the journey!

TRANSFORMERS RESCUE BOTS

Reading Adventures

LITTLE, BROWN AND COMPANY
New York   Boston

Little, Brown and Company

Hachette Book Group
1290 Avenue of the Americas, New York, NY 10104
Visit us at lb-kids.com

Little, Brown and Company is a division of Hachette Book Group, Inc.
The Little, Brown name and logo are trademarks of Hachette Book Group, Inc.

The publisher is not responsible for websites (or their content) that are not owned by the publisher.

First Hardcover Edition: June 2015
First Paperback Edition: June 2015

Meet Chase the Police-Bot, *Meet Heatwave the Fire-Bot*, and *Meet Boulder the Construction-Bot* originally published in 2013 by Little, Brown and Company.
Meet Blades the Copter-Bot and *Team of Heroes* originally published in 2014 by Little, Brown and Company.
Meet Optimus Primal originally published in 2015 by Little, Brown and Company.

ISBN 978-0-316-33747-2 (hc)—ISBN 978-0-316-28627-5 (pb)

Library of Congress Control Number: 2014952765

10 9

APS

PRINTED IN CHINA

Passport to Reading titles are leveled by independent reviewers applying the standards developed by Irene Fountas and Gay Su Pinnell in *Matching Books to Readers: Using Leveled Books in Guided Reading*, Heinemann, 1999.

Licensed By:

Meet Chase the Police-Bot...............7

Meet Heatwave the Fire-Bot...........37

Meet Boulder the Construction-Bot...67

Meet Blades the Copter-Bot............97

Meet Optimus Primal.................127

Team of Heroes.......................157

TRANSFORMERS
RESCUE BOTS

Meet Chase the Police-Bot

Adapted by **Lisa Shea**

Based on the episode
"Family of Heroes" written by
Nicole Dubuc

Attention, Rescue Bots fans!
Look for these words when you read
this book. Can you spot them all?

police car

wheels

museum

T. rex

I am Chase the Police-Bot.

I am part of a special group

of Transformers

called the Rescue Bots.

Optimus Prime gave us a mission
to serve and protect humans.
The other Rescue Bots are named
Heatwave, Boulder, and Blades.

I can turn into a police car.

My lights flash when I blast my siren.

I am fast on wheels!

I have a human partner.

His name is Chief Burns.

I enjoy working with the chief.

We do not let anyone break the law!

Chief Burns gets an alert.
The museum is on fire!
It is time for the Rescue Bots
to go on our first mission!

The museum has old stuff inside.
Boulder goes in to look, but I do not.
Chief Burns asks me to make sure
all humans get out safely.

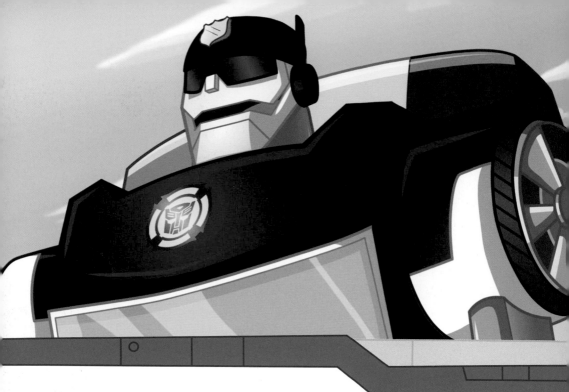

I do my job.

"Leave, please," I tell the humans.

"The museum is now closed."

I am very polite, and I do not yell.

But two humans do not respond.

Chief Burns calls them mummies.

When the mummies do not move,
I arrest them!

Chief Burns tells me
that the mummies can stay.
"We do not need to worry
about them, partner," he says.

Inside the museum,
a dinosaur robot
is about to fall on a human!
The chief runs in to help.

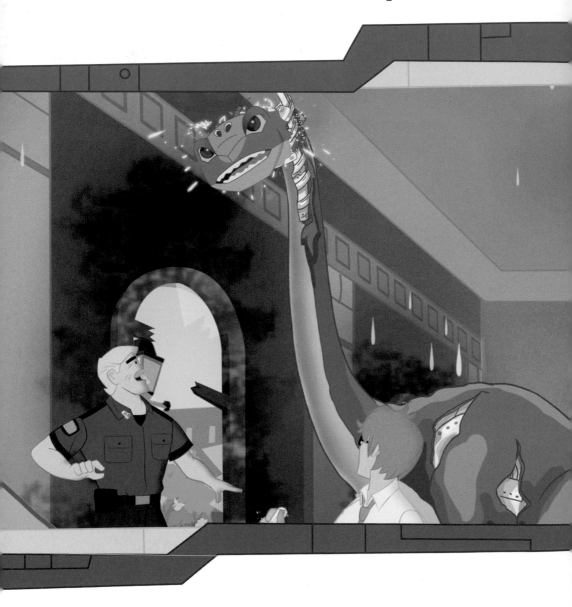

Heatwave is team leader
of the Rescue Bots.
He acts fast to catch the robot
and save both humans!

The Rescue Bots pretend
to be regular robots.
We are really alien life-forms.
Chief's family knows our secret.

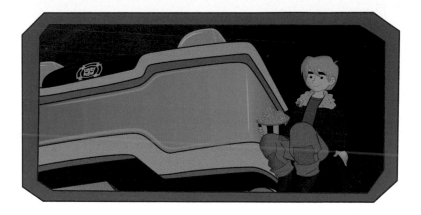

Chief Burns asks his son Cody
to help us hide in plain sight.
That night, Cody takes us to a movie
to learn about Earth.

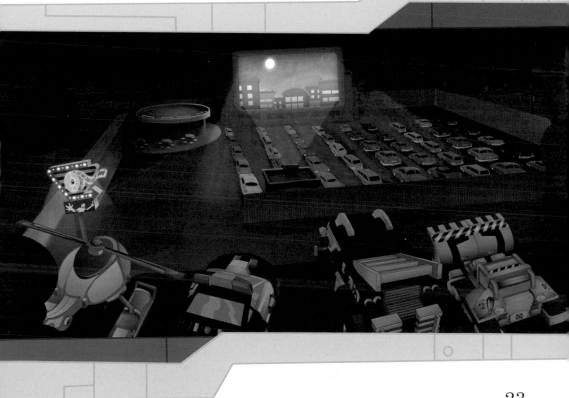

Blades sees something and asks,

"Is that part of the show?"

There is a T. rex robot on the loose!

It came from the museum.

"The fire messed up the wires

inside the robot," says Cody.

"Chase, turn on your lights!"
Cody tells me.
I flash my red and blue lights
and play my siren, too.

The T. rex turns around
and runs to me.
That is what we want.
We want it to leave the humans alone.

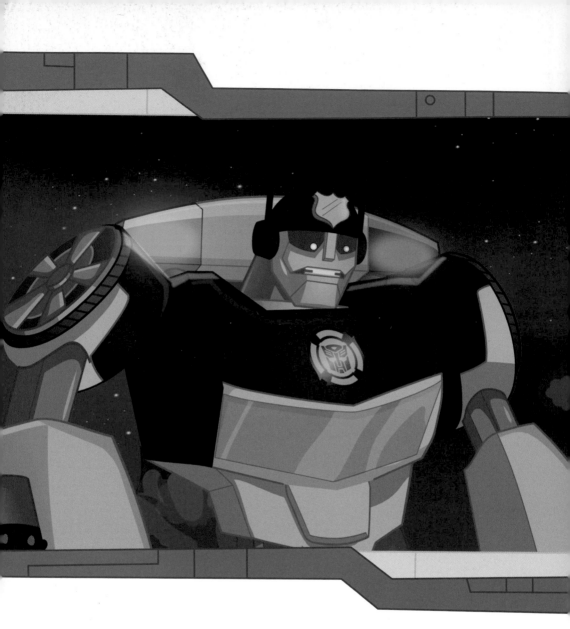

"Now what?" I ask.

To keep people safe,

we agree to lead the T. rex robot

to a place that has no humans.

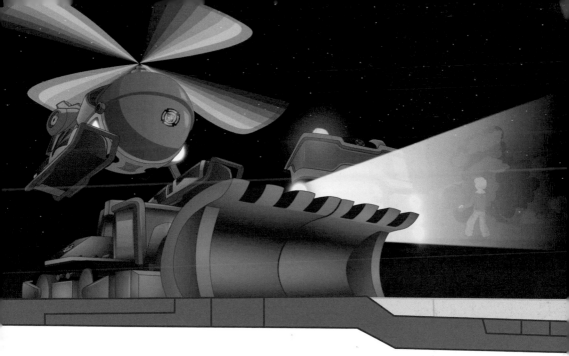

We change into our vehicles
and are on our way!
"Rescue Bots, roll to the rescue!"
says Heatwave.

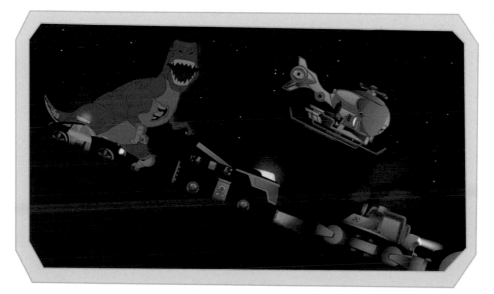

Blades needs to get a cage.

To give him time to do that,

I race around with lights flashing.

That keeps the dino bot busy.

Next, we need the T. rex to sit down.
Heatwave knows what to do.
He waits for the right moment
and then slams the T. rex into the mud!

Blades is back!

He drops a metal cage on the T. rex.

Cody sneaks up and flips a switch.

He turns off the robot's power!

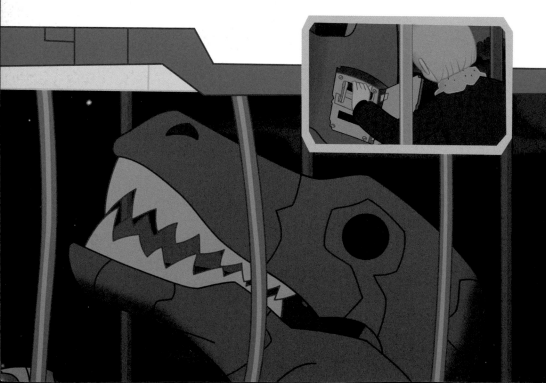

The chief is proud of Cody.

He puts him on the rescue team.

"I want a picture of all my heroes,"

he says as he takes a photo.

On the land, in the sky, or in the sea,
wherever there is an emergency,
there are the Rescue Bots!

Even if the emergency is just keeping humans cool on a hot day!

The Rescue Bots are always ready
to roll to the rescue!

TRANSFORMERS
RESCUE BOTS

Meet Heatwave the Fire-Bot

Adapted by **Lisa Shea**

Based on the episode
"Flobsters on Parade" written by
Brian Hohlfeld

Attention, Rescue Bots fans!
Look for these words when you read
this book. Can you spot them all?

fire truck

lobster

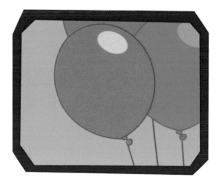

balloon

television

I am Heatwave.
I am the team leader
of a special group
called the Rescue Bots.

Optimus Prime gave us a mission
to serve and protect humans.
My team members are
Chase, Boulder, and Blades.

I change into a fire truck
and work with a human
named Kade.
Kade knows my secret.

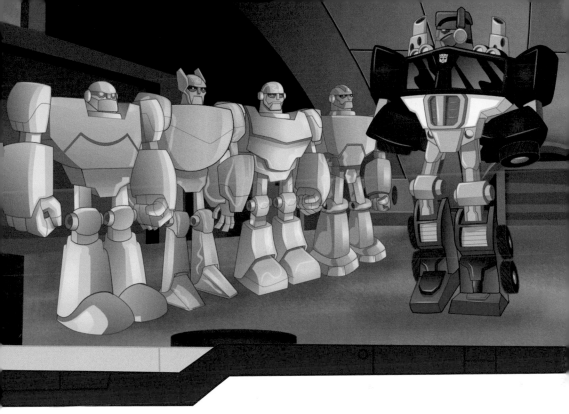

My secret is that I am an alien.

All the Rescue Bots are aliens.

We pretend to be

Earth robots to fit in.

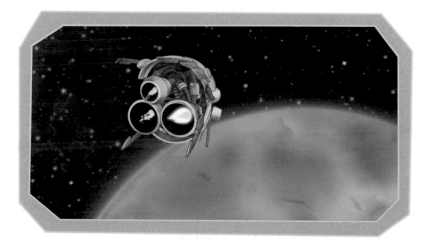

The town prepares for a parade.

Doc Greene fills a big balloon.

The balloon is shaped like a lobster.

Doc gets tangled up in a string

and floats away!

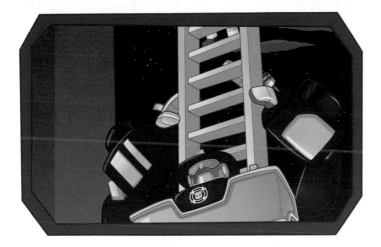

I know what to do.

My ladder goes up in the air.

Kade climbs up.

Together, we save Doc Greene!

Doc and his daughter Francine
thank Kade but not me!

Doc thinks I am a normal robot
and I do not have feelings.
That makes me mad.
I am not just a robot.

The next day,

our friend Cody teaches us a game.

It is called Simon Says.

"Simon says, lift your arms,"

Cody calls out.

We lift our arms.

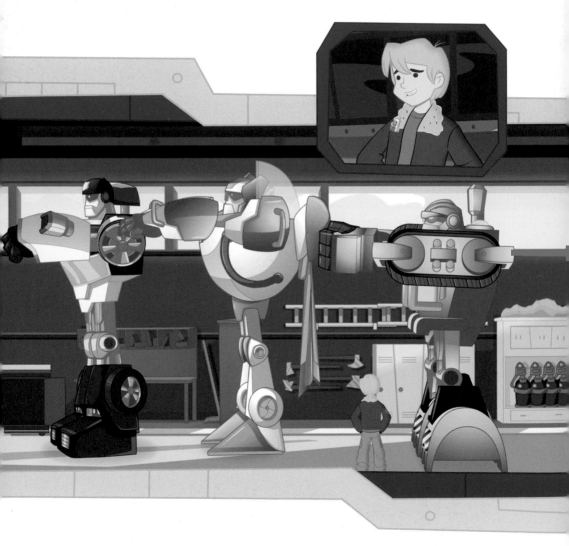

"Lift your left leg," Cody says.

Blades and Boulder lift their legs.

"He did not say 'Simon says,'"

Chase tells them.

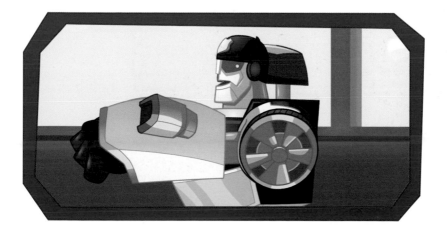

"That is right, Chase," says Cody.
"Remember to do only
what your humans tell you to do."
If we follow that rule,
we will seem like Earth robots.

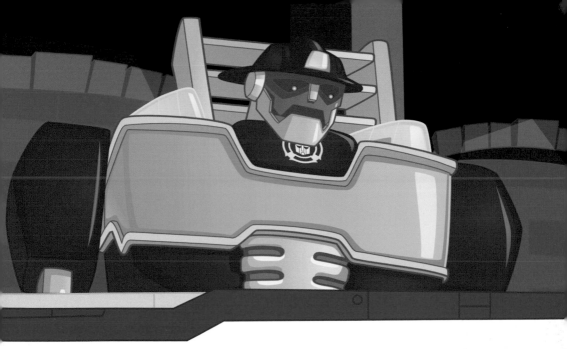

The Rescue Bots are going to march

in the parade.

We will pretend to be Earth robots.

I do not want to pretend.

"I will stay home," I say.

Cody tells me that

kids love to climb on fire trucks.

"One more reason not to go," I say.

"Human children are sticky!"

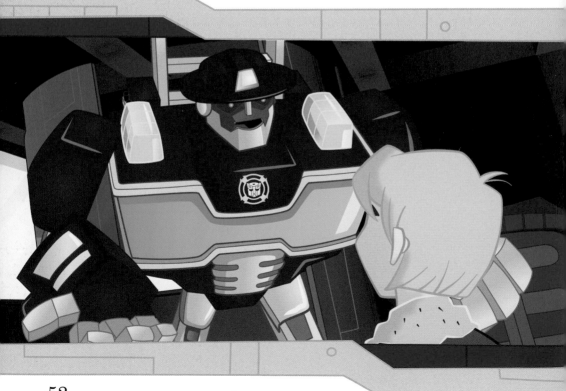

Chief Burns arrives to take
the Rescue Bots to the parade.
I pretend I am broken.
The group leaves without me.

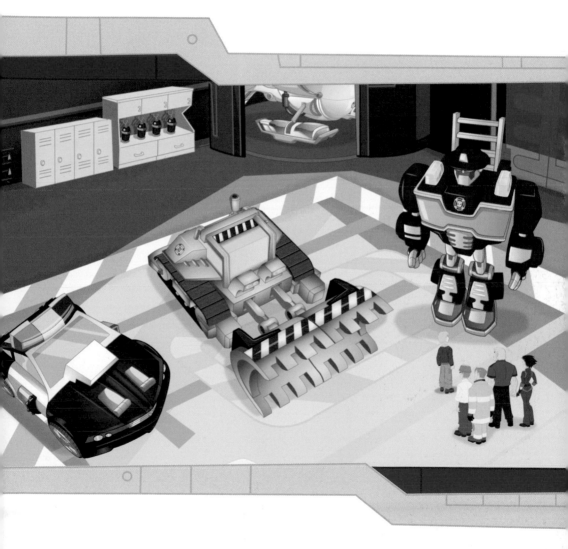

During the parade,

Doc Greene shows off a gas

he calls floatium.

Doc invented it to keep balloons

from floating away.

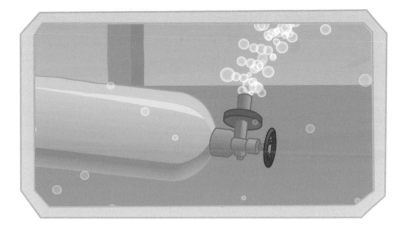

The floatium gas gets
into the lobster tank.
The lobsters start floating in the air!

Cody and Francine

think the floating lobsters are funny.

They call them flobsters!

"Oh, dear," says Doc Greene.
"The floatium will not wear off
for two more days!"
People try to jump
and catch the flobsters.

I am at home.

Kade calls me,

but I do not answer.

I am still feeling sorry for myself.

I turn on the television.

I see floating lobsters!

The flobsters attack the mayor

while he makes a speech!

The other Rescue Bots

do the best they can

to protect the humans.

I can see on TV that they still need help.

Lobsters like to eat starfish!
The flobsters think the starfish
on Francine's jacket is real.
She hides in a phone booth.

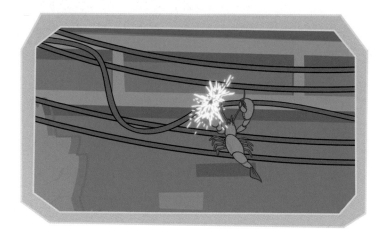

The flobsters attack!

I need to stop feeling mad.

My team needs me.

Kade needs me.

I rush into town to join the fight.
My fire hoses spray the flobsters
with massive water power.

The flobsters are afraid
of the giant lobster balloon.
We herd them into a trap
using the balloon.
I spray them back into the tank!

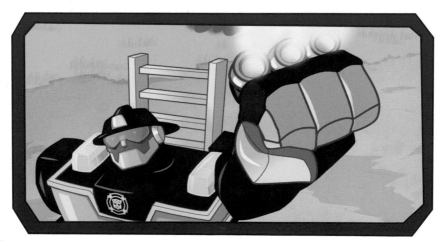

We saved the parade!

Everyone says

the Rescue Bots are heroes.

I feel so happy

I even let kids climb on me!

Kade whispers to me,

"You know you love it."

Guess what!

He is right!

Meet Boulder the Construction-Bot

Adapted by **Annie Auerbach**

Based on the episode
"Walk on the Wild Side" written by
Nicole Dubuc

Attention, Rescue Bots fans!
Look for these words when you read
this book. Can you spot them all?

cat

lion

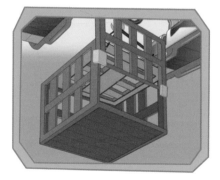

crate

plant

The phone rings in the firehouse.

"Emergency!

Come right away!"

the chief hears the caller say.

"It could be a fire!" says Dani.

"Or a broken pipe!" says Graham.

The Rescue Bots change form.

The humans jump inside and go.

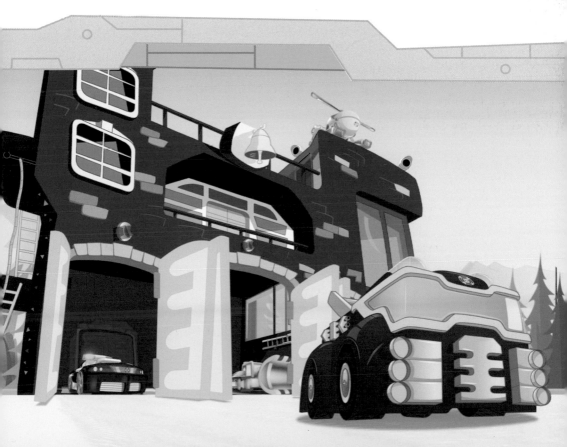

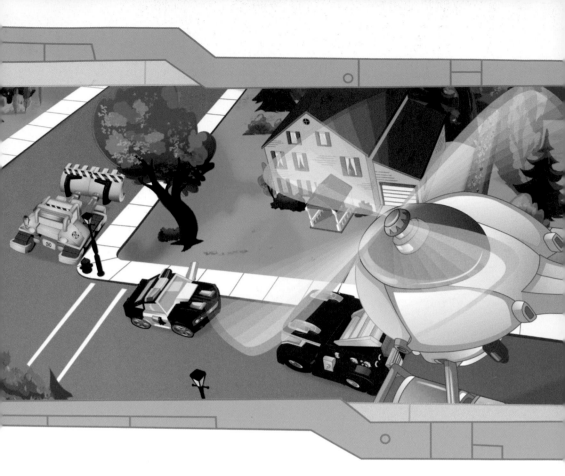

They arrive at a home.

What a surprise!

It is just a cat stuck in a tree!

Boulder changes back into a robot.
He helps the cat climb onto his body.
The owner is happy.

Later, Boulder asks Cody about pets.

Cody thinks pets are very cool.

"Some pets even work on rescue teams,"

Cody says.

"Wow!" says Boulder.

Now Boulder wants to get a pet
for the rescue team.
He wants it to be a surprise.
So Blades and Boulder sneak out at night.

Boulder wants to find a pet
at the zoo!

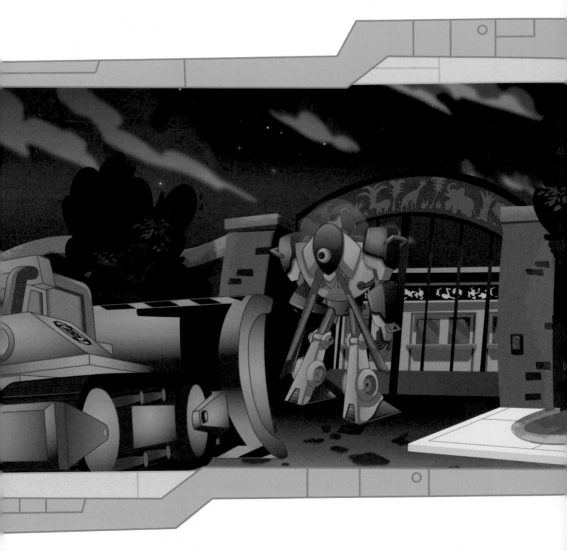

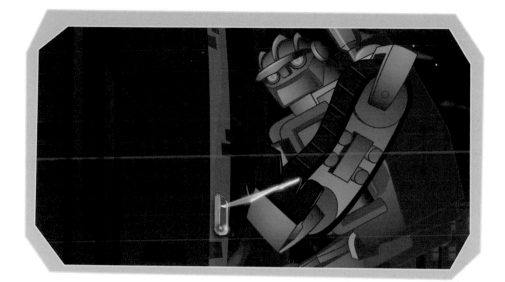

The gates are locked.

Boulder turns off the power.

The gates unlock

and all the cages open.

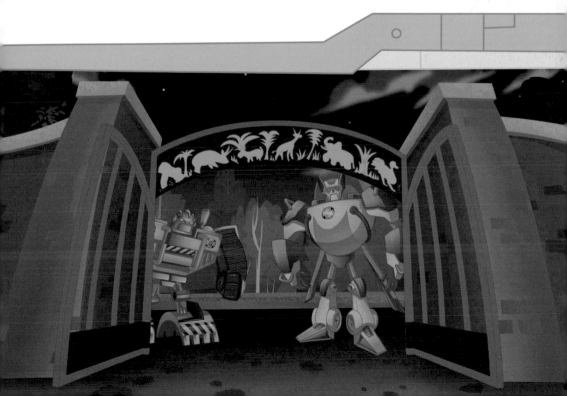

"Look!" says Boulder.

"Here is the perfect pet!"

He points to a large lion.

It reminds him of the cat
that he rescued.
"We can call it Whiskers,"
says Boulder.

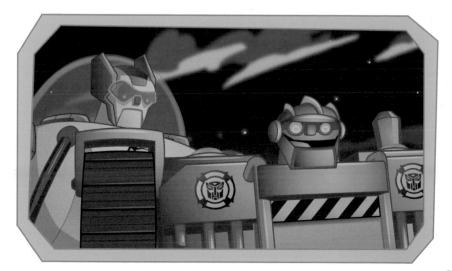

The lion roars.

It leaps out of its cage

and into a tree.

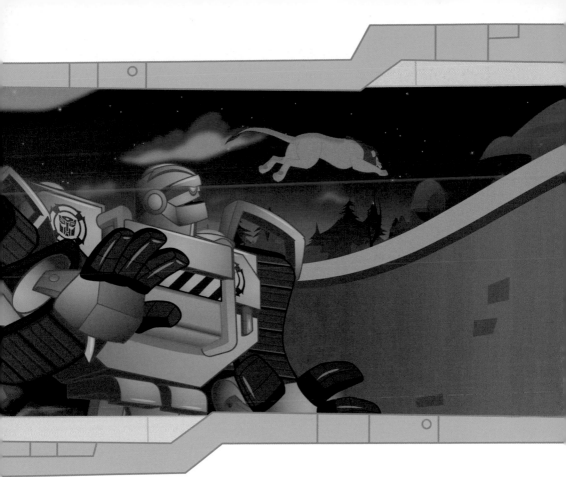

Then it jumps over the zoo wall.

The lion has escaped!

The next day,
Chief Burns gets a call for help.
He and the rescue team rush out
to find the lion in a tree!

"We found my pet!"

says Boulder.

"That is no pet,"

Graham says.

"That is a wild animal.

It needs to go back to the zoo!"

Boulder looks sad.

"Human ways are so confusing,"
says Boulder.

The lion jumps from the tree.

Chase tries to grab it but misses.

The animal runs down a busy street.

The team must catch the lion!

"Rescue Bots,
roll to the rescue!"
says Heatwave.

Boulder drives up on one side
of the lion.
Heatwave drives up on
the other side.

The lion snarls and growls.

It is trapped.

"Now!" shouts Graham.

Blades drops down a huge crate.

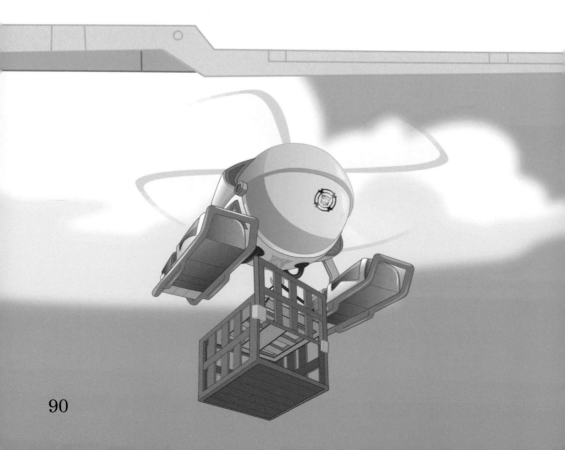

The lion is locked in the crate!

"Great catch!"

says Cody.

The animal is put back
in the zoo.
The mayor makes sure
the cage is locked.

"Whiskers was too much work,"
Boulder tells the team.
"But it would be nice
to have a pet."

"I know how you feel,"
says Cody.
"So I got you something
to care for."

Cody hands Boulder a plant.

"Come on, boy,"

Boulder says to the plant.

"Want to play catch?"

Cody laughs and shakes his head.

"Boulder!" he says.

"Plants do not play catch!"

Meet Blades
the Copter-Bot

Adapted by **D. Jakobs**

Based on the episode
"Under Pressure" written by

Nicole Dubuc

Attention, Rescue Bots fans!
Look for these words when you read
this book. Can you spot them all?

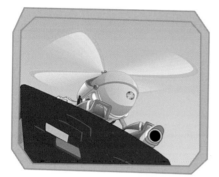

helicopter

volcano

lava

switch

Earth is very strange to the Rescue Bots.

Blades is having a hard time
in his new home.

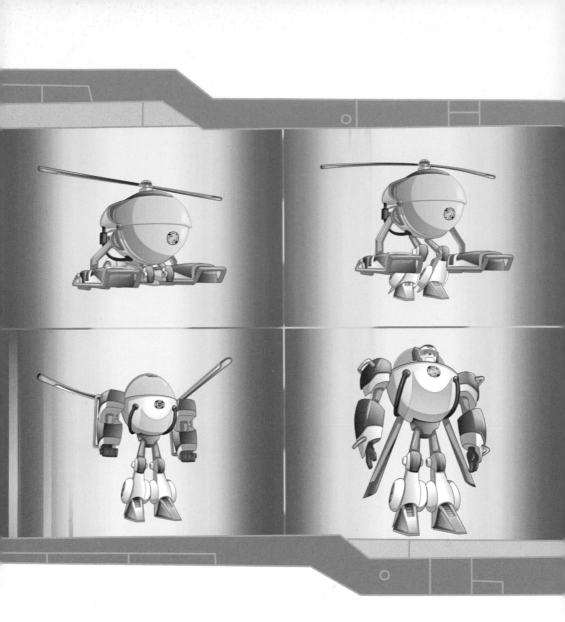

On Cybertron, Blades was a land vehicle.

He had wheels!

But here on Earth,

he changes into a helicopter.

Helicopters do not ride on the ground.

They fly!

Blades is scared of heights!

Blades has to be brave and fly
so he can do what
Optimus Prime told him.

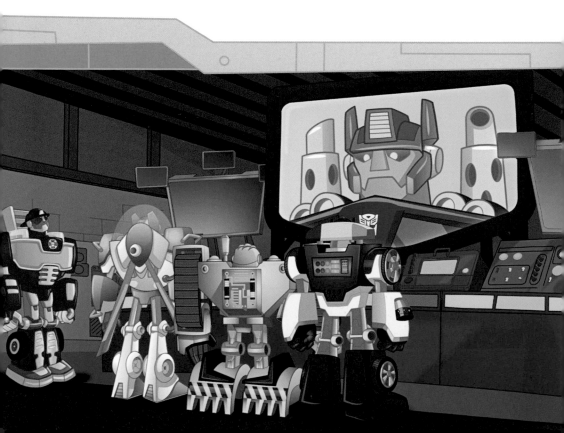

Blades's human partner, Dani, loves to fly.

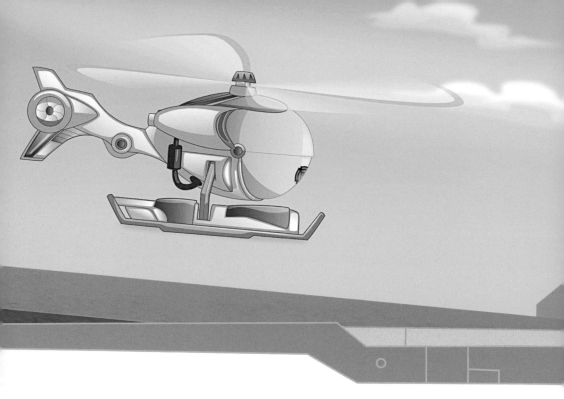

When they are flying together,
she pulls hard at his controls and yells at him.

"Hurry up, Blades!" she says.

"Go higher!"

Cody gets his family and the Rescue Bots together in the bunker.

He wants them to like and respect one another.

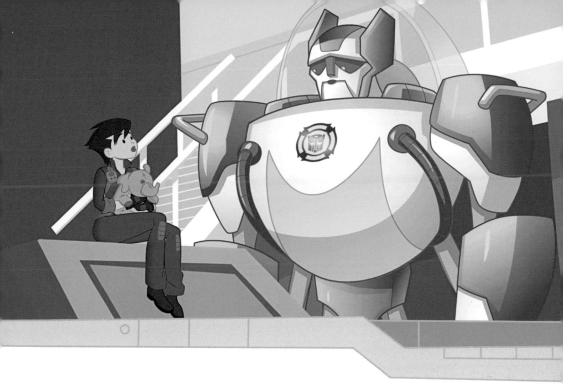

Blades and Dani try to be friends.

"Er, do you have any hobbies?" asks Blades.

"Flying," says Dani.

Blades does not like this answer.

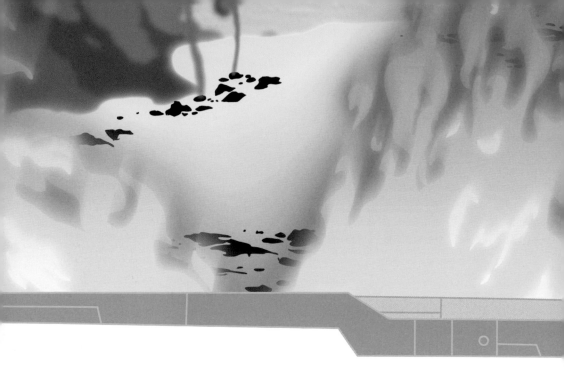

Just then, the town's fake volcano
starts erupting real lava!
Lava is rock that is so hot, it flows.
It can burn anything in its path.

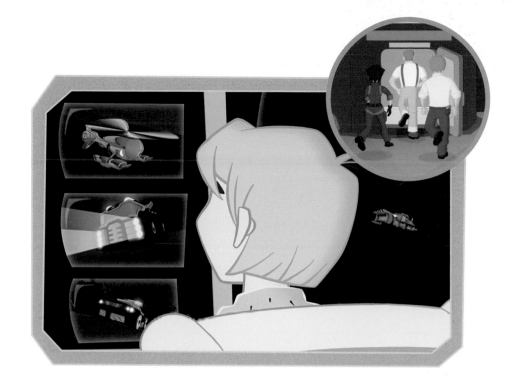

The team leaps into action.

Blades and Dani need to fly into the crater
and flip a switch before the volcano explodes.

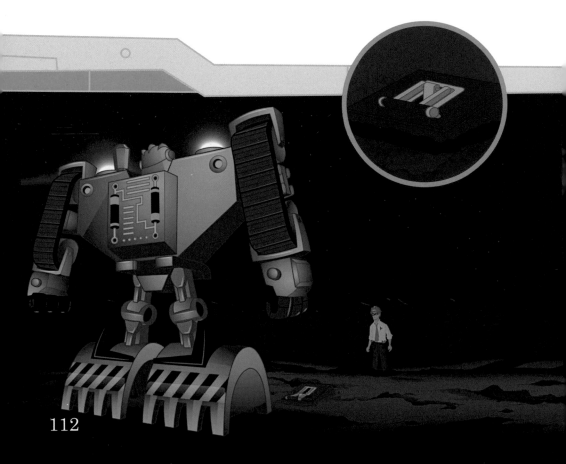

"Ow!

Can you be more gentle?" asks Blades.

"As soon as you learn to fly," says Dani.

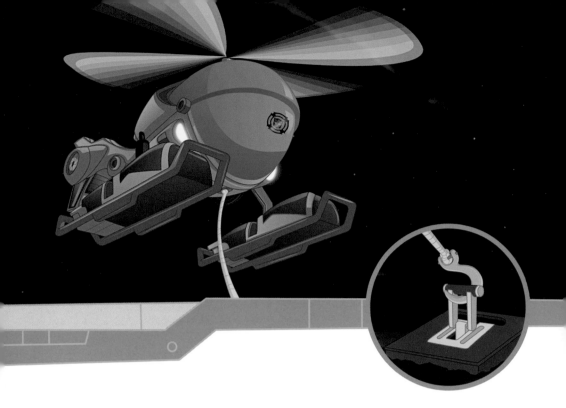

They need to fly fast and high.
The flying is scarier to Blades
than the lava, but he flips the switch!

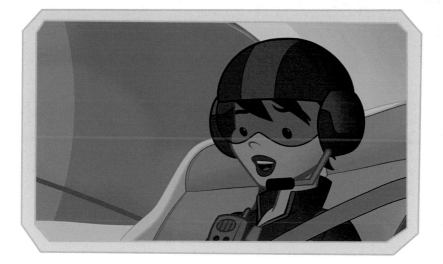

"We did it!" says Dani.

BOOM!

A cloud of ash bursts from the volcano.

Blades cannot see a thing!

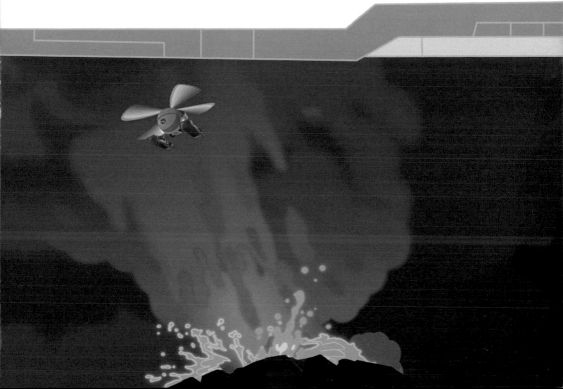

"Fly higher!" yells Dani.

"Which way is higher?" says Blades.

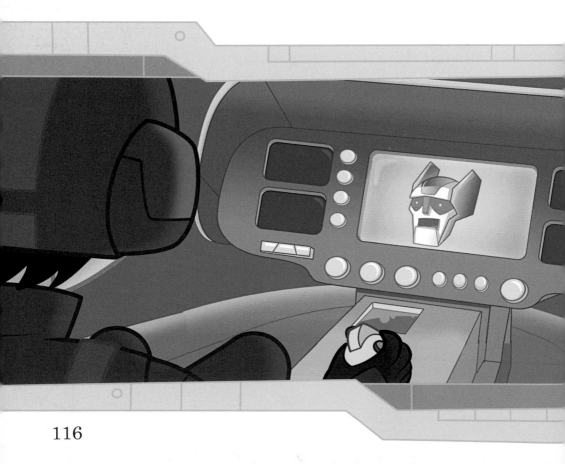

"Talk nicely to Blades, Dani,"
says Cody from the command center.

Dani and Blades work together

to get away from the ash and lava.

They are happy,

but the emergency is not over.

The leftover lava is heading down the tunncls toward Cody!

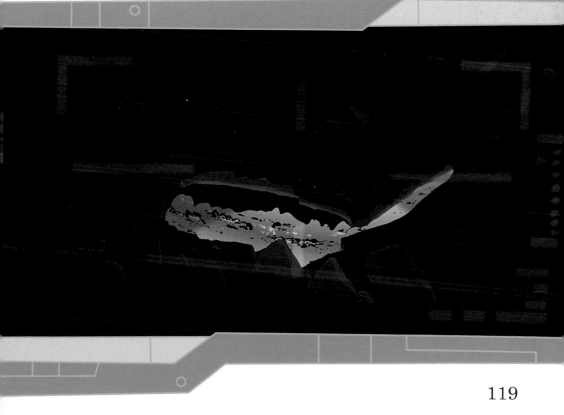

They need to cool the lava
and turn it back into rock quickly!

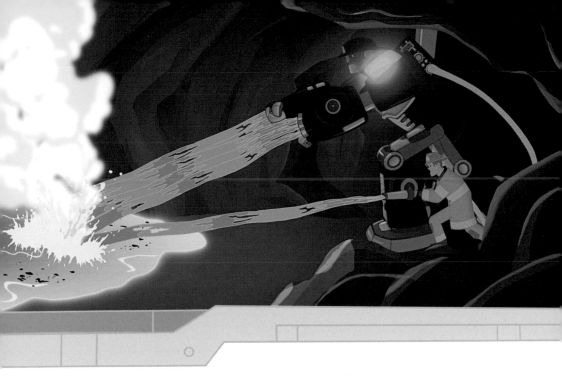

Heatwave and Kade try to stop the lava,
but the tanks run out of water.

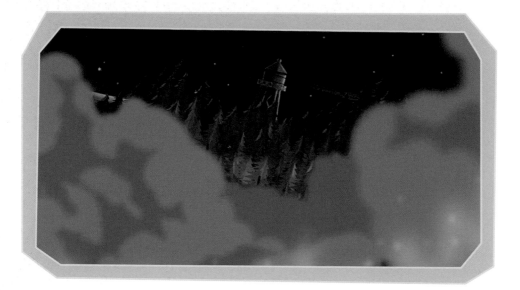

There is a huge water tower nearby,
but the ash cloud is in the way.
Only Blades can get there in time.

"The ash may hurt your rotors," says Dani.

"It is worth it to help Cody!" says Blades.

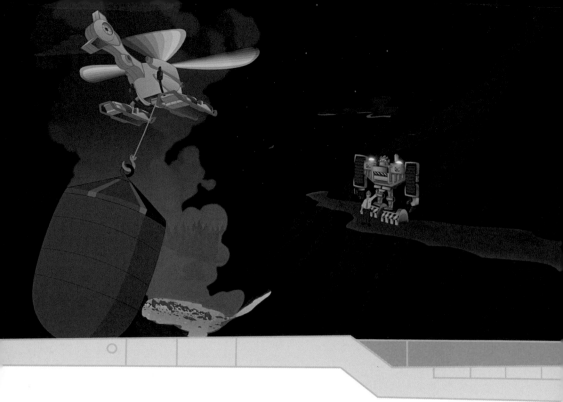

With Dani's help,
Blades soars through the smoke
and picks up the water tower.
Together, they save the day.

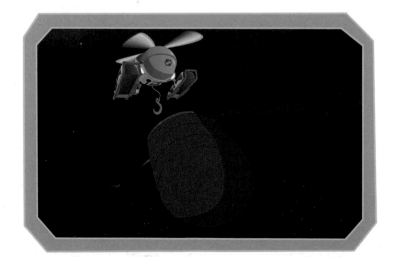

"We did it, partner!" says Dani.

They both feel very proud.

Blades finally feels at home.

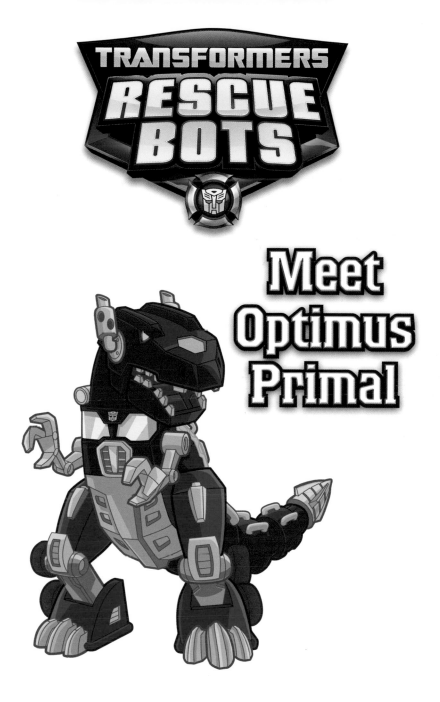

TRANSFORMERS RESCUE BOTS

Meet Optimus Primal

Adapted by **Jennifer Fox**
Based on the episode "Big Game"
written by **Greg Johnson**

Attention, Rescue Bots fans!
Look for these words when you read
this book. Can you spot them all?

truck

hunter

blaster

frozen

Optimus Prime is the brave
leader of the Rescue Bots.

Boulder, Chase,
Heatwave, and Blades
are his team.

Optimus Prime can change
from a robot . . .

...into a powerful truck
that can even travel underwater!

He can also change into...

...Optimus Primal!
This is his dino mode.
He is a T. rex.

In dino form, Optimus Primal
takes his friend Cody
for a wild ride.

"Hold on!" Optimus shouts.

He races across the grass.

Optimus Primal roars!

His roar shakes the trees.

A greedy hunter named
Colonel Quarry sees Optimus Primal
in the forest.

"A dino bot!" the hunter shouts.

Colonel Quarry chases Optimus.

He wants to catch him.

Optimus has another idea.

He chases the hunter!

The hunter reaches
for his blaster.

Optimus stomps on it
with one mighty foot.

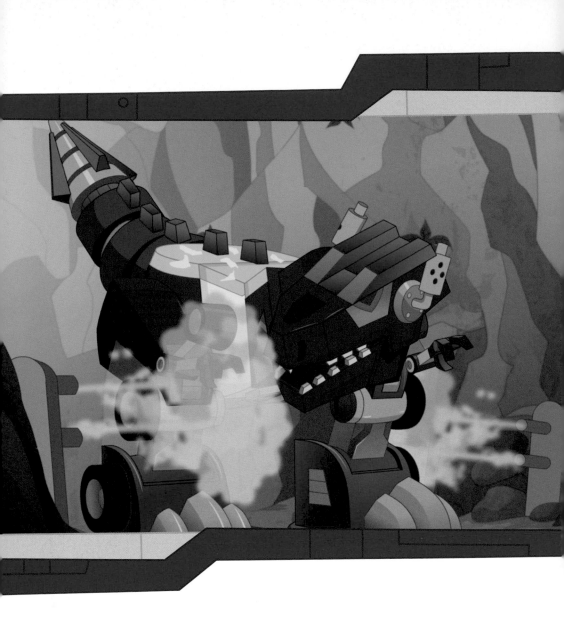

The hunter set a trap.

Icy mist covers

Optimus and Cody.

Optimus Primal is frozen!

"It is c-c-cold!" says Cody.

Boulder rushes to the rescue.

"I have your back!"

the Rescue Bot calls.

Boulder brings the hunter's Heli-jet

to the ground.

Boulder changes into dino mode.
He is now a triceratops.

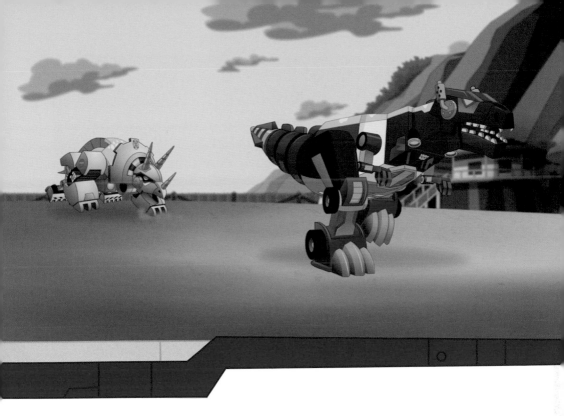

The hunter is getting away!
Optimus and Boulder charge
to stop him for good.

They catch the hunter!

Optimus brings his pal Cody
back home.

Optimus Prime is a strong leader
and protects humans.

He is even stronger with a great team
like the Rescue Bots!

Optimus Prime
and the Rescue Bots
are always there
for one another!

TRANSFORMERS RESCUE BOTS

Team of Heroes

by Jennifer Fox

Attention, Rescue Bots fans!
Look for these words when you read
this book. Can you spot them all?

Earth

human

lava

car

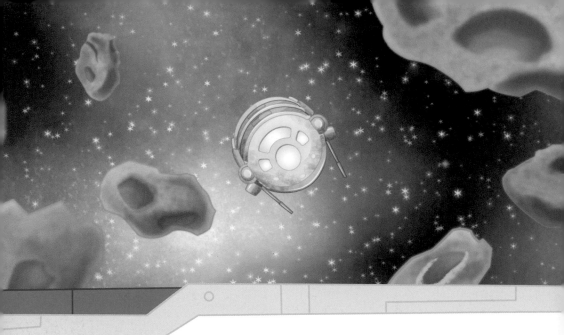

A new class of Autobots

lands on planet Earth!

They are the Rescue Bots.

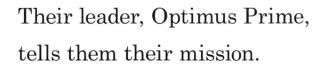

Their leader, Optimus Prime,
tells them their mission.

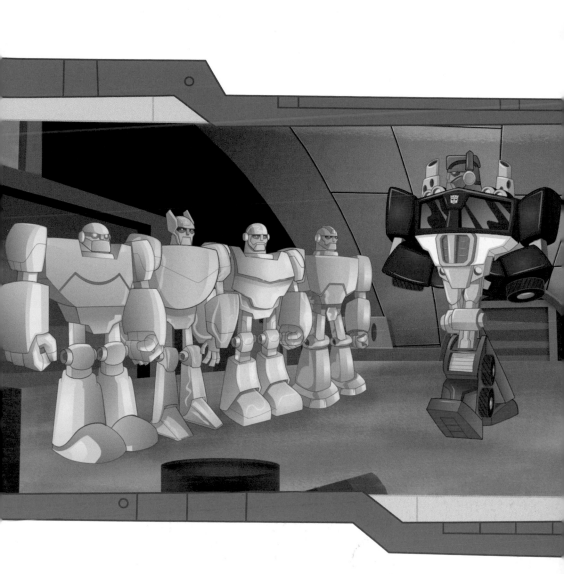

"Work together
with the humans.
Serve and protect," he says.

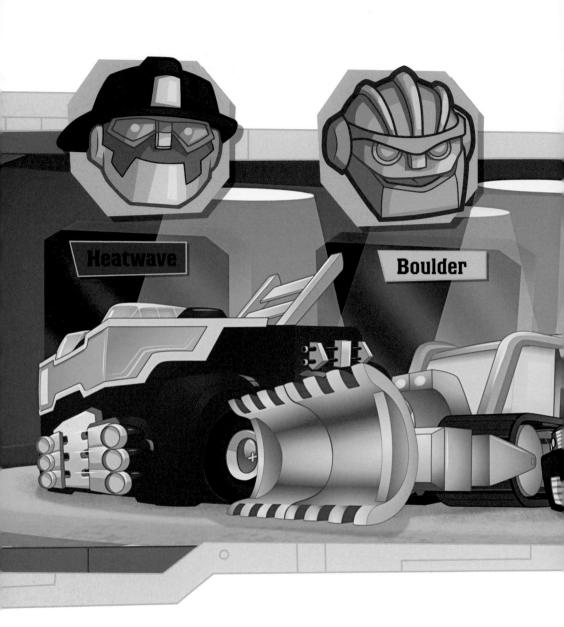

The Rescue Bots choose vehicle forms
that will help them
be a great rescue team.

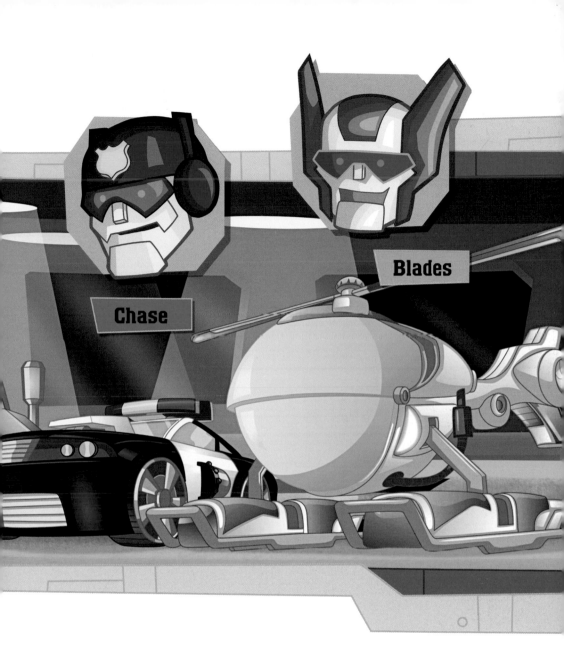

Chase

Blades

Heatwave, Boulder,
Chase, and Blades
are ready to roll out!

The Rescue Bots will work
with Chief Charlie Burns.

The human is the leader
of Griffin Rock Rescue.

Chief Burns's family will help, too.

Cody is the youngest Burns.

He is a great dispatcher.

Kade played football in school,
and now he is a firefighter.

Dani is the chief's only daughter.

She enjoys action and danger.

She is a tough pilot.

Graham is smart and steady

in any tricky situation.

He is an engineer.

Cody calls the team.
They need to gather
for a mission.

"There is trouble on the roads,"
he tells them.

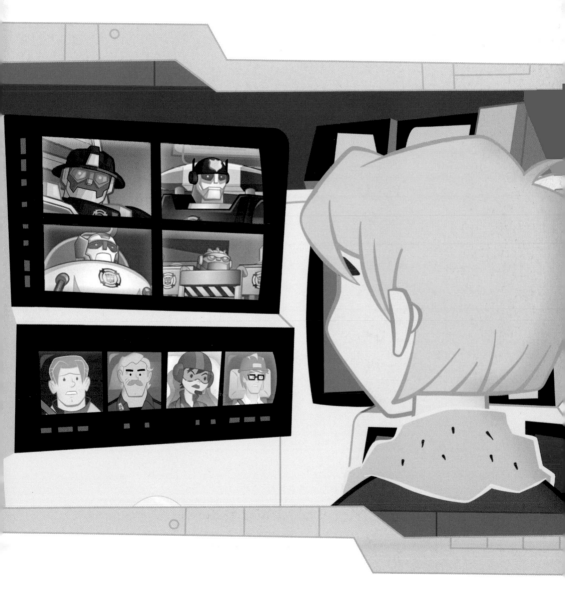

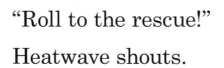

"Roll to the rescue!"
Heatwave shouts.

The Rescue Bots change
into their vehicle forms.
They roll out to save
the people of Griffin Rock.

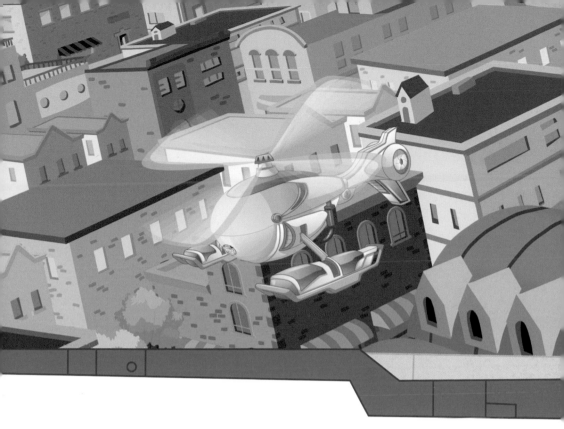

Dani and Blades fly high
to get a better look.

A bridge is out!
Kade and Heatwave
rush into action.

They save a man
from the raging river.

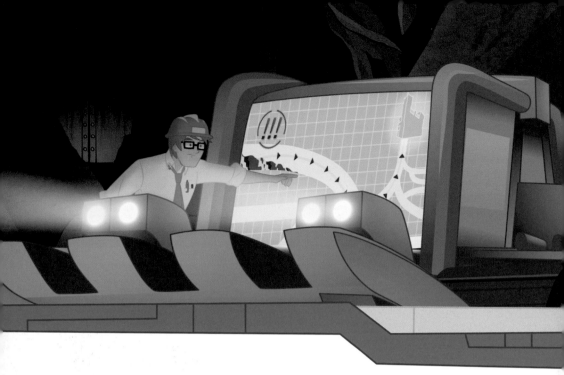

Boulder and Graham
find a hot problem—
a lava leak!

The town is in danger,
but the Rescue Bots
show no fear.

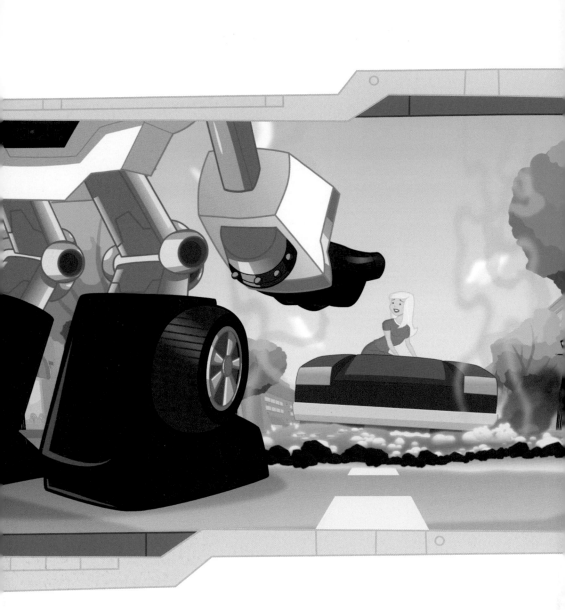

A car skids into
a lava puddle.

But Chase is on the scene!
He scoops up the driver, Hayley,
just in time.

The rest of the team stop the lava.

Chief Burns says, "Mission accomplished!"

The streets are safe again.

Chief Burns is proud
of his family.

He is proud of the Rescue Bots, too.

The rescue team
knows what it takes
to get the job done:
teamwork!

The End

Roll to the rescue with the

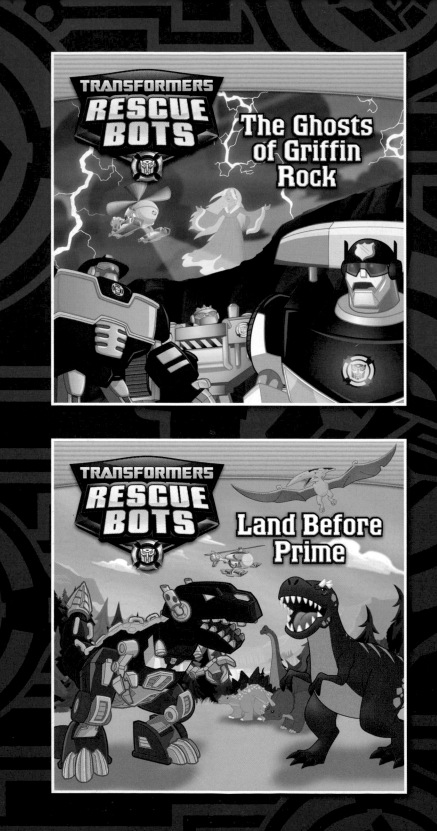

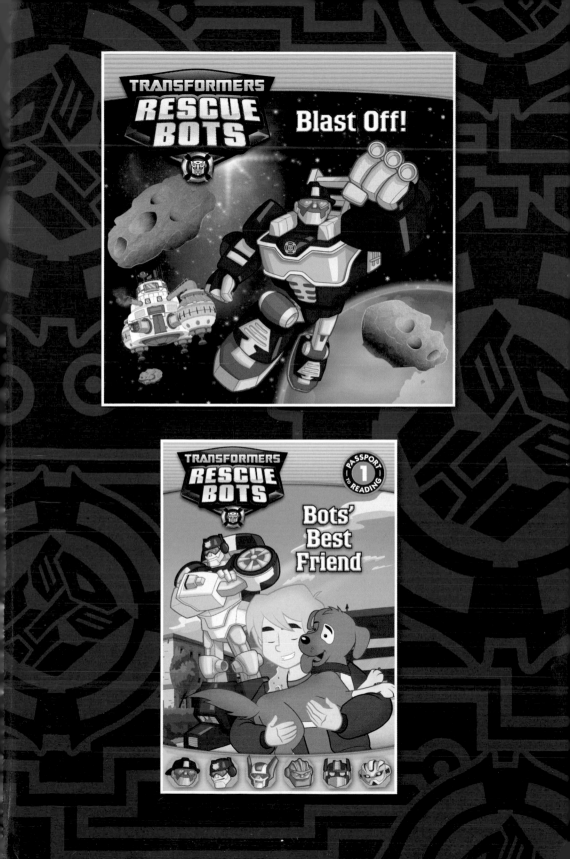

CHECKPOINTS IN THIS BOOK ✔

Meet Chase the Police-Bot

WORD COUNT	GUIDED READING LEVEL	NUMBER OF DOLCH SIGHT WORDS
547	J	92

Meet Heatwave the Fire-Bot

WORD COUNT	GUIDED READING LEVEL	NUMBER OF DOLCH SIGHT WORDS
547	K	92

Meet Boulder the Construction-Bot

WORD COUNT	GUIDED READING LEVEL	NUMBER OF DOLCH SIGHT WORDS
426	I	81

Meet Blades the Copter-Bot

WORD COUNT	GUIDED READING LEVEL	NUMBER OF DOLCH SIGHT WORDS
423	J	76

Meet Optimus Primal

WORD COUNT	GUIDED READING LEVEL	NUMBER OF DOLCH SIGHT WORDS
239	J	43

Team of Heroes

WORD COUNT	GUIDED READING LEVEL	NUMBER OF DOLCH SIGHT WORDS
293	I	54